The Wishing Balloon

Written by
Kim Berry

Copyright © 2024 by Kim Berry. 858645

All rights reserved. No part of this book may be reproduced or transmitted in any form or by any means, electronic or mechanical, including photocopying, recording, or by any information storage and retrieval system, without permission in writing from the copyright owner.

This is a work of fiction. Names, characters, places and incidents either are the product of the author's imagination or are used fictitiously, and any resemblance to any actual persons, living or dead, events, or locales is entirely coincidental.

To order additional copies of this book, contact:
Xlibris
844-714-8691
www.Xlibris.com
Orders@Xlibris.com

Library of Congress Control Number: 2024906447
ISBN: 979-8-3694-1901-4 (sc)
ISBN: 979-8-3694-1900-7 (hc)
ISBN: 979-8-3694-1902-1 (e)

Print information available on the last page

Rev. date: 04/19/2024

This book is dedicated to
Kaitlyn and Patrick,
who are my dreams and wishes
that came to me.

Love always,
Mom

"Come on, guys. It's time to leave," said Mom.

Patrick and Kaitlyn came running to the car,

Patrick with his blue balloon and

Kaitlyn with her birthday gift bags.

"The birthday party was so much fun," said Patrick.

"Thanks," said Kaitlyn.

"My swimming birthday party this year was a blast!"

As they drove off in the car,

Patrick pointed to the sky and said,

"Kaitlyn, good thing
your party is over.

The sky is starting to look
like it might rain."

Kaitlyn looked up at the sky and shouted excitedly,

"Look! A full rainbow! It's right in front of us!"

"I see it too!"

"Look at all the beautiful colors!"

"Do you know what rainbows are made of?" Mom asked.

"No," Patrick and Kaitlyn said curiously.

"What are rainbows made of?"

"Well," said Mom, "every time a balloon slips

out of someone's hand, it soars with the wind

way up into the sky, traveling to the wishing place."

"What happens at the wishing place is magical.

All the red balloons line up in red,

all the orange balloons line up in orange,

all the yellow balloons line up in yellow,

all the green balloons line up in green,

all the blue balloons line up in blue,

and all the purple balloons line up in purple."

"But before the wishing balloons can go to

the wishing place, a person must make a wish

while the balloon is sailing high up into the sky."

"When the wish has been asked for, the balloon

joins all the other wishing balloons at the magical

wishing place behind the clouds,

and together they make beautiful rainbows."

"Every time we see a rainbow, it means

many people are getting their wish at that moment."

When they reached home,

Kaitlyn got out of the car with some of her birthday gifts

and Patrick with his blue balloon.

Suddenly, Patrick closed his eyes and opened his fingers, and his

balloon started to climb high into the sky.

"Make a wish!" said Mom and Kaitlyn excitedly.

"I have," replied Patrick with a smile.

So Kaitlyn, Patrick, and Mom held hands

as they watched the balloon find its way to

the wishing place.

"Goodbye to the wishing balloon," they said.

"We will see you in the next rainbow."

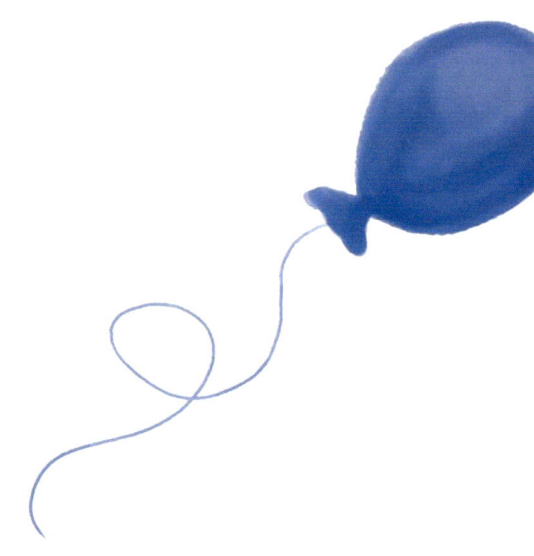

The End